This book belongs to

· ·

D1438557

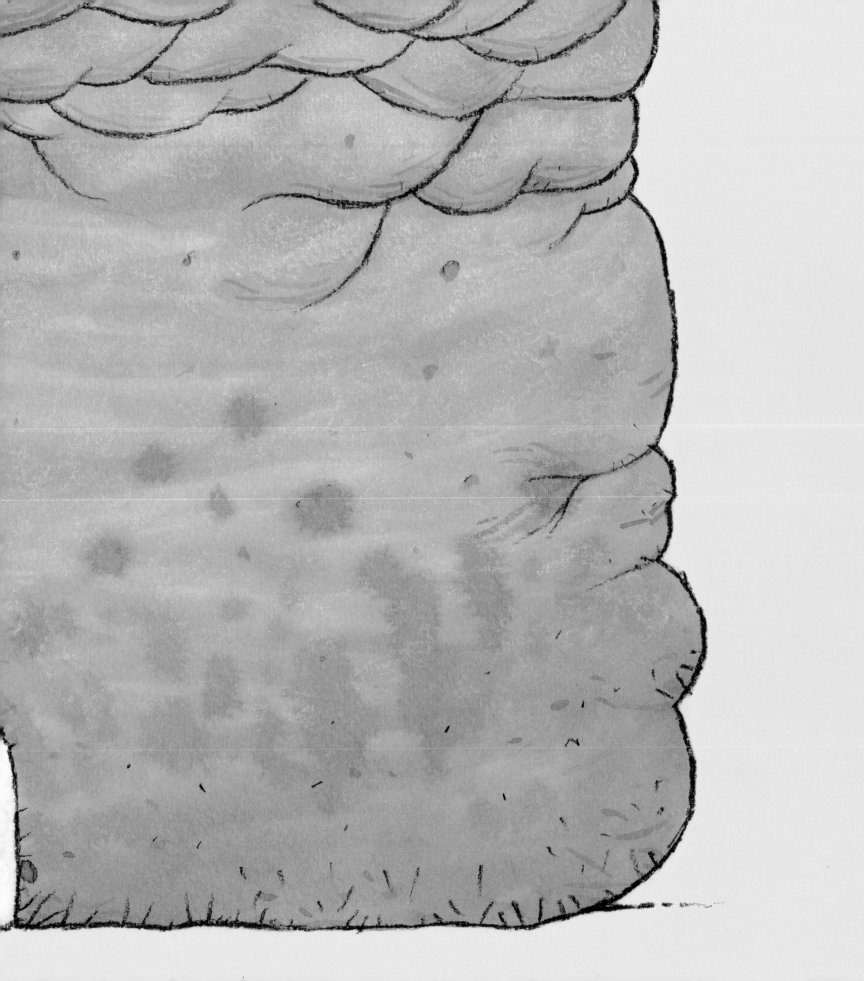

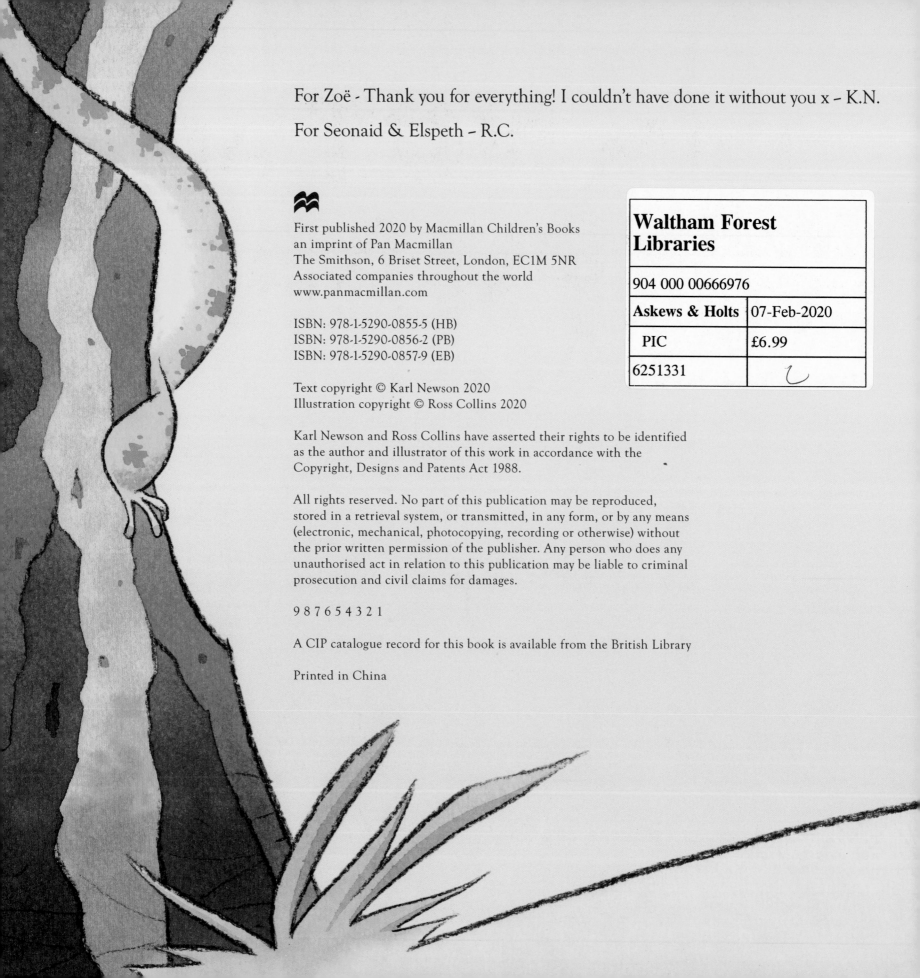

For Zoë - Thank you for everything! I couldn't have done it without you x – K.N.

For Seonaid & Elspeth – R.C.

First published 2020 by Macmillan Children's Books
an imprint of Pan Macmillan
The Smithson, 6 Briset Street, London, EC1M 5NR
Associated companies throughout the world
www.panmacmillan.com

ISBN: 978-1-5290-0855-5 (HB)
ISBN: 978-1-5290-0856-2 (PB)
ISBN: 978-1-5290-0857-9 (EB)

Text copyright © Karl Newson 2020
Illustration copyright © Ross Collins 2020

9 8 7 6 5 4 3 2 1

A CIP catalogue record for this book is available from the British Library

Printed in China

I AM NOT AN ELEPHANT

KARL NEWSON **ROSS COLLINS**

MACMILLAN CHILDREN'S BOOKS

Hello,
elephant!

I am **NOT** an elephant.

You **ARE**! You've got an elephant's pointy nose.
You've got an elephant's flappy ears.

PAH!!

No. Not I.

I am *not* an elephant.
An elephant **PARPS**, but *I* do not . . .

I GROWL
like an owl . . .

GRRR-IT
T-WRR!

I BEEP
like a sheep . . .

BAA-
EEEP!

I QUACK
like a yak . . .

I MEOW
like a cow . . .

ME-OOo!

KWAK!

I AM NOT A SM·ELEPHANT!

I'm a mmm . . .
melon.

I'm small, round
and tasty.

BAH! NO!

I am **NOT TASTY** at all!
I taste horrible!

YUCK!

I'm a . . . mooo . . . se.

NO YOU'RE NOT!

You don't look anything
like a moose!

Maybe not.

But, it's what's on the inside that counts,
don't you think?

Or you'd be
a brush.

And you,
a gherkin.

I AM a moose
and I am . . .

AMAZING!

And you, madam,
an umbrella.

PARP!

HA! What a silly old bunch.

Now – at last – it's time for lunch!

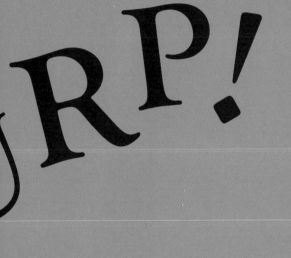

URP!

GAH! I'm NOT a moose.
No, not anymore!

Did you hear my **ROAR!?**

Yes! I'm a . . .

DINOSAUR!

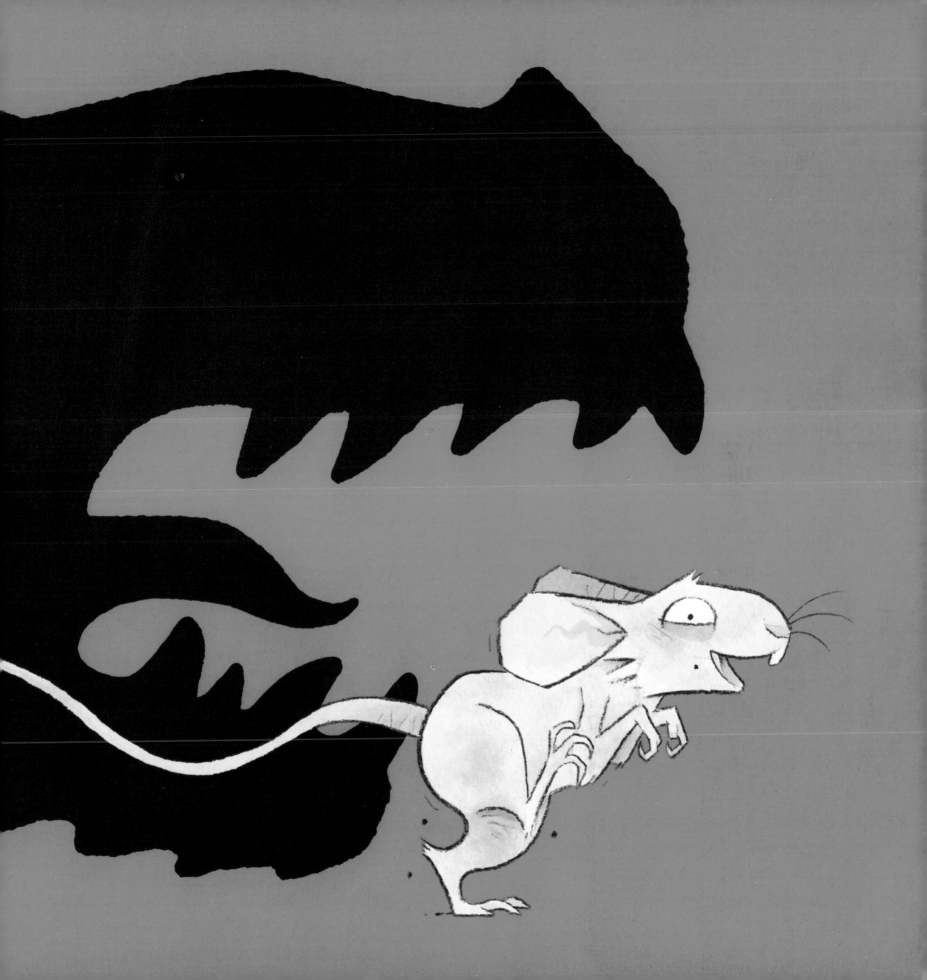

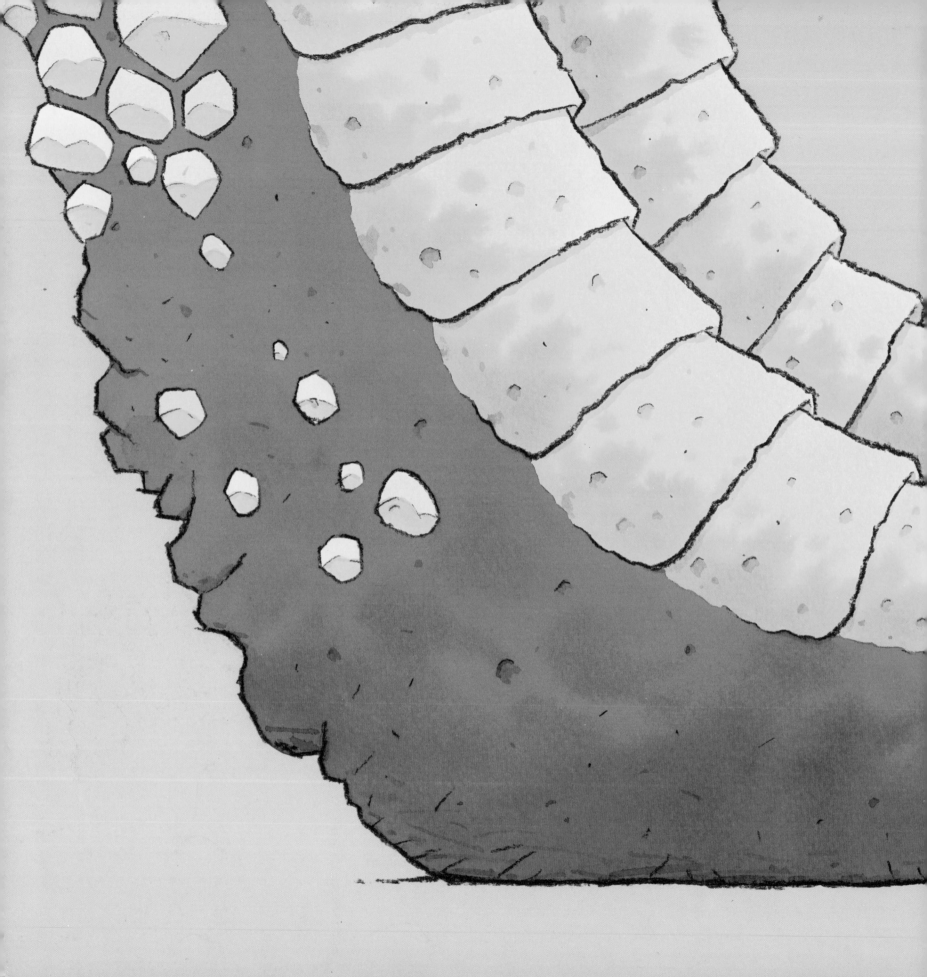